the WIDE-MOUTHED FROG

written and illustrated by Rex Schneider

Stemmer House
PUBLISHERS, INC.
Owings Mills, Maryland

Inquiries should be directed to
Stemmer House Publishers, Inc.
2627 Caves Road
Owings Mills, Maryland, 21117

Printed and bound in Hong Kong

First printing 1980

Second printing 1989

A Barbara Holdridge book

Designed by Barbara Holdridge
Color separations by National Colorgraphics, Inc.,
    New York, N.Y. and Capper Inc., Knoxville,
    Tennessee
Composed in Souvenir Medium by Typesetters, Inc., Baltimore,
    Maryland
Printed on 86-pound matte art paper and bound by Everbest
    Printing Company, Hong Kong/Four Colour Imports,
    Ltd., Louisville, Kentucky

Library of Congress Cataloging in Publication Data

Schneider, Rex.
    The wide-mouthed frog.

    SUMMARY: A wide-mouthed frog asks advice of the
other animals in the Okefenokee swamp on proper diet.
Then he meets an alligator who eats only wide-mouthed
frogs.
    [1. Frogs—Fiction. 2. Animals—Fiction. 3. Diet
—Fiction. 4. Okefenokee Swamp—Fiction] I. Title.
PZ7.S3642Wi   [E]   80-13449
ISBN 0-916144-58-5
ISBN 0-916144-59-3 (pbk.)

Once there was a Wide-Mouthed Frog
who lived in the great Okefenokee Swamp. His
mouth was very wide indeed, and he took enormous
pride in it.

He was so proud
that he would spend whole days admiring his
reflection in the water. He thought he must be the
most extraordinary creature in the whole swamp.

Soon the Wide-Mouthed Frog
began to think himself too grand to eat lowly bugs
like mosquitoes and flies.

One morning, before the
sun was up, he jumped onto a very high branch and
croaked for all to hear,

"I'm a Wide-Mouthed Frog,
in need of food grand enough
for such a Frog as me."

"Well, I'm a Long-Eared Bat,"
squeaked a voice overhead, "and I say you make
too much noise! Go ask the Owl—maybe she can
give you advice. Bugs are good enough for me!"

The Wide-Mouthed Frog searched,
and soon found the Owl. "Oh Owl, I am a Wide-
Mouthed Frog. Can you tell me what food is noble
enough for such a creature as me?"

"Well, I am a Great Horned Owl,
and my favorite food is mouse. But I hardly think
that would be good enough for you. Why not ask
the Oppossum?"

"Oh, 'Possum, 'Possum,"
called the Frog. "What food is most glorious for a
Wide-Mouthed Frog like me?"

"Well, I'm the New World Opossum,
and for me there is nothing as fine as a nice, fresh
egg. But it may be that the Deer can suggest
something more to your liking."

Off hopped the Frog,
and found the Deer at dinner. "Oh Deer, I'm the
Wide-Mouthed Frog, in search of food fit for me to
eat. What do you recommend?"

"Well, since I am the Great White-Tailed Deer, the best foods I know are the tips of branches and wild roses. But these would hardly do for you. The Egret might have better choices."

"Oh Egret, Egret,
I am the Wide-Mouthed Frog, come to ask what
food is dainty enough for me to eat."

"And I am the Great White Egret,
and I very much prefer fresh fish. But I can see it's
not for you. Go wake up the Turtle with your
questions!"

So he swam further still.
"Oh Turtle, guide me to a dinner fine enough for a
Wide-Mouthed Frog to eat. What do you suggest?"

"Well, I am the Eastern Box Turtle,
and mushrooms are just fine for me. As for you,
maybe the Raccoon can suggest the proper diet for
a Wide-Mouthed Frog."

The Raccoon seemed happy to assist,
when the Frog asked him his question. "Best,
indeed? Well, being a common Ring-Tailed
Raccoon, I like nothing better than a crayfish
dinner. But this would hardly do for you. Perhaps
you should see the Squirrel?"

The Squirrel heard his name
and listened. "Oh Squirrel, I'm the very beautiful
Wide-Mouthed Frog, in search of something special
enough for me to eat. What do you think is best?"

"Well, I am only the Southern Flying Squirrel, after all. Pinecones are just fine for me, but surely not for you. I wonder if the Fox, who knows a thing or two, can help you out."

On swam the Frog,
and soon he found the Fox. "Oh Fox, I need your
help. I am the very bright and beautiful, sleek and
strong Wide-Mouthed Frog, and cannot find food
good enough for me to eat. What am I to do?"

"Well, I'm the Wily Red Fox,
and if I were you, I would ask the King of the
Swamp, the Alligator, for his exalted advice."

The Wide-Mouthed Frog searched
and searched, until he found the Alligator gliding
through the waters of the swamp. "Oh, your
Majesty, King Alligator, I've come to you at last. I'm
the Wide-Mouthed Frog, and I need to know what
food is good enough to eat."

"Well, I am the Mighty Great American Alligator, and I think that the very best food of all is a WIDE-MOUTHED FROG."

"OH,"
said the little-mouthed frog.

Then, before the Alligator could come any closer,
he hopped away with all his might, smaller and
smaller and smaller. And suddenly he was
dreadfully hungry for a big fat mosquito or fly.